JUMP SERVE

BY JAKE MADDOX

illustrated by Tuesday Mourning

text by Bob Temple

Librarian Reviewer
Chris Kreie
Media Specialist, Eden Prairie Schools, MN
MS in Information Media, St. Cloud State University, MN

Reading Consultant
Mary Evenson
Middle School Teacher, Edina Public Schools, MN
MA in Education, University of Minnesota

STONE ARCH BOOKS
Minneapolis   San Diego

Jake Maddox Books are published by Stone Arch Books,
A Capstone Imprint
1710 Roe Crest Drive
North Mankato, Minnesota 56003
www.capstonepub.com

Library of Congress Cataloging-in-Publication Data
Maddox, Jake.
    Jump Serve / by Jake Maddox; illustrated by Tuesday Mourning.
    p. cm. — (A Jake Maddox Sports Story)
    ISBN 978-1-4342-0470-7 (library binding)
    ISBN 978-1-4342-0520-9 (paperback)
    [1. Volleyball—Fiction. 2. Teamwork (Sports)—Fiction.]
I. Mourning, Tuesday, ill. II. Title.
PZ7.M25643Jum 2008
[Fic]—dc22   2007031262

Summary: Ella and Laura can't believe it when two of the meanest girls
from a rival volleyball team switch to their team. They decide to give the
girls a chance, but before long it's clear that Beth and Gretchen have no
plans to be good teammates. Since Laura has been benched with a knee
injury, Ella feels very alone on the court. How can she manage to get
Gretchen and Beth to play with her, not against her? Is there any hope
for a championship, or was the season ruined before it began?

Art Director: Heather Kindseth
Graphic Designer: Kay Fraser

Printed in the United States of America in Stevens Point, Wisconsin.
102012
006960R

TABLE OF CONTENTS

CHAPTER 1
The Jump Serve

Ella held the ball carefully in her hands. She knew the time was right.

Her team was leading 24–23. Ella knew that this serve could be the final point of the game.

The winning serve here would mean a trip to the championship for Ella's volleyball team, the Rockets.

Ella got ready for the serve.

"Come on, El, let it rip!" cried Laura, Ella's best friend.

Ella looked over at her. Laura, the team's best setter, stood in the middle of the court, cheering her teammate on.

"If you're not going to do it now, when are you?" Laura yelled.

Ella knew what Laura was talking about. A jump serve.

Ella had a powerful serve from a standing position. But she had also been practicing a jump serve.

Standing back from the end line, she would run up, flip the ball into the air, leap, and power the ball over the net like a bullet. When the serve was on target, it was difficult to stop. It could decide a game easily.

Very few girls her age could do a jump serve. The other team might not be ready to handle it. That would work in Ella's team's favor.

There was only one problem. Ella knew her serve wasn't perfect yet.

If it didn't work, they might not get the point. And then they wouldn't win.

Laura still wanted her friend to try it. Laura yelled, "Come on, Ella!"

Ella took a deep breath. She tried to turn off the noise of the crowd and forget the stares on her. She just focused on the way the volleyball felt in her hands.

Finally, she was ready. She stepped back from the line.

Thud. Thud. She bounced the ball twice.

Then she held it out in front of her in her left hand. She stared it down.

Then she pulled it back in and bounced it twice more.

Thud. Thud.

Finally, Ella held it out in front of her again. She always started a serve that way. She thought it brought her luck.

She stepped forward and tossed the ball into the air. Then she leaped up and pounded the ball with the palm of her right hand.

The ball whizzed across the net. It barely cleared the tape. It was headed for the floor, and it was staying in bounds!

A player from the other team ran across the floor. She dove for the spot the ball was targeting, but she was too late.

It was a great try, but the ball fell off the ends of her fingers and rolled across the floor.

The Rockets had won!

Ella leaped into the air.

Laura and the rest of her teammates rushed to her. They jumped up and down, hugging and giving each other high fives.

"We're going to the championship match!" Laura yelled.

Ella beamed with pride.

She had played very well, but she was especially proud that her new skill, the jump serve, had won the match.

As they walked off the court, the girls noticed that their rivals, the Lakers, had been watching from the stands.

The Rockets would play the Lakers in the championship match the next day.

Two players from the Lakers stepped forward. "Enjoy it while you can," one of them said. "Tomorrow, we're definitely going to beat you."

CHAPTER 2
Fear Factor

Ella and Laura laughed off the threat. They both had played against the Lakers girls many times before, and it was always like that.

The Lakers were always trying to scare the other teams. If they weren't whispering mean things about the players on the other team, they were loudly telling people that they were going to beat them.

Usually, they were right.

The Lakers were the best volleyball team in the area. They hardly ever lost. When they did, it was usually a shock.

The Lakers even traveled outside the area for tournaments. They played in regional and sometimes even national events.

The Rockets were a younger team. They hadn't been playing together as long. They didn't have the same winning record as the Lakers.

But the program was getting better every year. This year, the Rockets had started to beat some of the top teams.

The match against the Lakers would be the Rockets' first tournament championship match so far that season. Ella and Laura were thrilled, but nervous.

The Rockets had played in several other tournaments. They had come close to going to the championship match a couple of times, but they had not made it.

Ella and Laura were excited that they were playing in the finals at a tournament. But they knew their chances weren't great against the Lakers.

* * *

The next morning, the Rockets gathered on the court. They began their warm-up for the match.

The Rockets had warm-up routines that they did before each match, but they were nothing at all like the routines that the Lakers did before a match. The Lakers' warm-up routines were famous through the entire league.

Watching the Lakers warm up before a match was like watching an army get ready for battle. The players yelled cheers and chanted the whole time.

The routine got the Lakers ready to play, and it made other teams nervous. The Rockets, watching, could tell that they were in for a difficult match.

When the match finally started, the Rockets were pretty shaky. The Lakers quickly won the first game of the match without any trouble.

The Rockets felt horrible afterward. During the break between games, the Rockets' coach tried to settle the upset players down.

"Girls, you're acting like someone just kicked your dog," Coach Stiggle said.

She smiled at the players. "It's not that serious. It's just a game. Now go out there and have fun. Do the best you can."

That made the girls feel more relaxed. They headed back out to the court feeling braver and more confident.

The second game was better. Laura did a great job as the setter. She passed to Ella for kill after kill.

It was a hard game. Finally, in the end, the Rockets were able to pull out the victory.

Ella served for the winning point, but this time, she held off on the jump serve. She wanted to save that for the third game.

CHAPTER 3
Final Game

The Lakers started serving at the beginning of the third and final game of the championship match. They quickly scored five points in a row. That gave them the early lead.

The Rockets players tried to not get too disappointed. After all, the game wasn't over yet. They finally took the serve back when Laura set the ball for Ella, who spiked it for a point.

That got the Rockets on the scoreboard. They finally felt like they really had a good chance to compete for the championship title at the tournament. There was no reason they couldn't win the game if they played their hearts out.

Both Ella and Laura were at the top of their games. They were both playing incredibly well that day. And even more importantly, they were playing really well together.

As the setter, Laura's job was to feed the ball to the team's hitters. The hitters would leap and try to spike the ball for kills.

Being the setter was a great job for Laura. She wasn't nearly as tall as the other girls, so she wouldn't work well as a hitter.

Ella was tall, and she could jump really high. She was perfect for her role as a hitter. Like Laura, she had practiced a lot to improve her skills.

Ella was quickly becoming one of the best hitters in the league. It felt great to have her hard work paying off.

Laura and Ella were best friends. They practiced a lot together, and that helped them on the court.

Laura knew exactly where Ella was going to be and exactly how to set the ball to her. Ella knew how to time her leaps to meet Laura's sets in the right place. They made a great team.

During the third game of the match, Ella and Laura were pretty sure that the Lakers were a better team than they were.

The Rockets were having trouble taking the lead. Every time they tied the score, the Lakers would get the next point. The Lakers would get three or four points ahead.

Then the Rockets would work their way back into the match and tie the score.

It kept going like that for the whole game. Each team would get a few points, and then the other team would catch up.

Near the end of the third and final game, the Lakers led 24–22. It was their turn to serve.

Laura took her position near the net. She got ready for the serve.

Once the serve was on their side of the court, Laura would try to play it to Ella. Then Ella would spike it. That could keep the game alive.

Laura bounced a little on the balls of her feet. She waited for the serve. But before the serve came, Laura heard one of the Lakers players call out to her.

"I hope you guys had fun," the girl said, "because it all ends here." It was the same girl who had teased Laura and Ella the day before.

Laura kept quiet. It wasn't worth arguing with the girl. She knew the girl was just trying to make her nervous.

Soon, the serve came. Carrie, another girl on the Rockets, kept the ball alive.

Then Laura moved into position. She set the ball toward the net, where Ella would get to it.

Ella ran over. She pounded the ball to the ground on the Lakers' side of the court.

The score was 24–23. The Rockets had the serve.

It was Carrie's turn to serve. She powered the ball over the net.

The Lakers returned it. Then Carrie sent the ball in Laura's direction.

Laura knew that it was their chance. A good set and spike could tie the game. Then the Rockets would have a real chance to win.

But the ball was a little high for Laura, and off to one side. Still, she jumped up. She knew what she had to do. She needed to get the set up toward Ella.

Laura got her fingertips on the ball, but she wasn't in the right place. She couldn't control its path. She tried, but the ball didn't move the way she wanted it to.

The ball moved toward the net. Ella ran to try to keep it in play.

Just as Ella reached the ball, she heard Laura cry out.

Ella tapped the ball and it landed out of bounds on the other side of the floor.

Laura crumpled to the ground in pain.

CHAPTER 4
Recovery

The game was over.

The Lakers had won.

The Lakers players jumped up and screamed and cheered. The Rockets girls all looked sad. They stood around the court trying not to show their disappointment.

Ella didn't care that they'd lost. She just cared about Laura. She rushed to Laura's side.

Laura clutched her knee. She wasn't crying, but she looked like she might start any second.

Ella hugged her friend. "You'll be okay, Laura," she told her.

Ella and Coach Stiggle helped Laura get off the court. They sat her down on the bench. Coach Stiggle went to call Laura's parents.

While the rest of the girls went to shake hands with the Lakers, Ella stayed with Laura on the team bench.

The Lakers players went through the line. Then two of them walked over to Ella and Laura.

"It's too bad you girls are such bad losers," one of the girls said. "You can't even shake hands and congratulate us?"

"She's hurt," Ella said. "She can't stand up." She looked around for Coach Stiggle, but she was on the other side of the court talking on a cell phone.

"If you say so," the other girl said. "It looks to me like she's a bad loser, though," she added. Her friend laughed. Then they turned and walked away.

* * *

Later that day, things got even worse. Laura's doctor shook his head when he saw her injury.

"I'm sorry, Laura," he told her. "You've torn some ligaments in your leg. This is going to take a while to heal."

"I'll be able to play for the rest of the season, right?" Laura asked nervously. "I mean, this won't keep me off the court?"

The doctor sighed. "You will play again," he told her. "But you'll have to have an operation first, and then go through physical therapy to make sure your knee heals properly."

"So . . . when will I be able to play?" Laura asked. Tears were starting to fill her eyes. She had a bad feeling about this.

The doctor sighed again. He looked upset. "Well, Laura," he began, "if you work hard, you will be able to play again by the middle of next year's volleyball season."

Laura burst into tears for the second time that day.

When she got home from the doctor's office, she called Ella to tell her the bad news.

"I tore up my knee pretty bad," Laura said. "The doctor said that I'm not going to be able to play for a while."

A tear rolled down Laura's cheek. "I can't believe this is happening," she said.

"Don't worry, Laura," Ella said. "You'll be back on the court before you know it."

* * *

The season soon came to an end.

Laura had an operation to repair her knee. Then she began physical therapy.

Three times a week, she went to a special clinic, where she learned exercises that would help her knee heal. She had to perform the exercises at home, too.

All winter long, she worked hard to get her knee back in shape to play.

Laura's doctors told her she wouldn't be able to play until the middle of the next season. The Rockets would have to start the season without her.

At first, that was okay with Laura, because she knew she would be back to play soon. She planned to go to practices and help out, but not play. That meant at least she'd be able to hang out with Ella.

But as the season drew nearer, Laura got sad. She wanted to be able to play, not just sit on the sidelines and help their coach.

One night just before the season started, Ella called Laura.

"I have a great idea," Ella said. "Seriously, you're going to love it."

Laura laughed. "Of course you have a great idea," she said.

Ella ignored her. "Since you're going to come to practice, you could help me work on my spikes," she said happily.

Laura was confused. What did Ella mean? "Ella, the doctors said I can't play," she reminded her friend. "How am I supposed to help you?"

Ella laughed. "You can just stand on the court and pass balls to me at first. But as your knee gets better, you can do more! What do you think? I can't stand to think of a season where we don't play together!"

Laura smiled. Finally, she was excited about the volleyball season again. "I think it's a great idea," Laura replied.

* * *

On the first night of practice, Laura's mom dropped her and Ella off at the gym.

They strolled up to the doors and swung them open.

When they looked inside, they couldn't believe their eyes. There, wearing Rockets warm-ups over their practice uniforms, were those two girls from the Lakers.

Ella and Laura didn't know what to say. They looked at each other, shocked. Then they walked over to Coach Stiggle.

"Um, Coach?" Laura said. "What are those girls doing here?"

"Yeah," Ella added, "and why are they wearing our colors?"

"Simple," Coach Stiggle said, putting down her clipboard. She smiled. "They're Rockets now."

CHAPTER 5
New Teammates

Ella's athletic bag hit the floor.

Laura's mouth dropped open wide.

"What?" they said together.

"Girls, we get new players on our teams every year," Coach Stiggle said. She put her hands on her hips and frowned. "You've never reacted like this before," she added.

"We've never had Lakers move to our school before," Laura muttered.

Coach Stiggle shook her head. "Laura, they're Rockets now. Gretchen and Beth have both moved into our district this school year. It's not that big of a deal. And these girls are really good players. They can help us get to the next level."

She looked at Ella and Laura and said, "I know you'll both be welcoming. That's what I expect from my team — especially from two of my best players."

"Okay," Ella said quietly.

Ella sat down and started to put her volleyball shoes on. Laura did the same. She had to be careful not to stretch her knee too far.

They talked very quietly. "Can you believe this?" Laura whispered. "How are we going to play with these girls?"

"I don't know," Ella said, "but it doesn't look like we have much choice. I guess all we can really do is try to be good teammates."

Before Laura could respond, the two new girls walked over to them. They had changed into their Rockets practice clothes. Ella thought it was strange to see their rivals wearing the same thing she and her teammates were.

"Is there a problem, girls?" one of them said.

Ella and Laura looked at each other. Then Ella stood up. She held out her hand. "Nope," she said quickly. "No problem. We're just surprised to see you here, that's all." Ella was trying her best to be friendly. It wasn't easy.

"Well, we are here," the taller girl said, flipping her hair back. "I'm Gretchen. This is Beth. I hope you're ready to play this game the right way now. We're here to help the Rockets win some championships."

Gretchen's attitude was already annoying Laura. "We did just fine without you," Laura said.

Gretchen glanced down at the brace on Laura's knee. "Oh, yeah, I remember you," Gretchen said with a laugh. "When we beat you, you wouldn't even shake hands with us. Real nice."

Beth pointed at Laura's knee and gave a small, mean laugh.

"I guess I won't have much competition to be the setter, will I?" Beth said. "It looks like you won't be playing for a while."

Laura narrowed her eyes. Ella could tell her friend was mad, so she tried to calm everyone down.

"Hey, listen," Ella said. "I know we were rivals before, but we're on the same team now. We might as well try to get along."

There was a long pause. All the girls stared at each other.

Finally, Ella spoke again. "Anyway, welcome to the Rockets," she said. "We're happy to have you on our team."

Gretchen smirked. "This isn't your team anymore," she said. "It's our team now."

CHAPTER 6
Not the Same

For the first four weeks of the season, the Rockets practiced hard. They were working on all of their techniques and skills to get ready for the tournament season. That meant Ella was spending a lot of time on the court with Gretchen and Beth.

During practices, they got along okay. For the most part, Ella kept to herself. She didn't want either girl to say anything mean to her.

Since Beth was the setter, she worked with both Ella and Gretchen, setting them up for spikes.

Ella thought Beth was a good setter, but she wasn't as good as Laura.

Laura was excited, because her knee was starting to feel better. The physical therapy was down to only once a week, and her knee felt better every day. She knew that after a few more weeks, she'd be able to start playing again.

When the first tournament rolled around, Ella was nervous. She wasn't sure how it was going to go, especially since she had two new teammates in the picture.

Ella had gone out of her way to be nice to the new girls, but they hadn't exactly been nice back.

Beth and Gretchen didn't talk trash to Ella's face anymore, but she did keep overhearing them whispering, and they also rolled their eyes during practice a lot.

To make things worse, they never cheered on their teammates. They didn't even celebrate with the team after a good practice.

The Rockets opened their season's first tournament with a match against a team called the Blazes.

At the start of the first game, the Rockets jumped out to a 5–0 lead. Ella hadn't gotten a chance for a kill, but she could tell it was going to come. The Rockets were clearly the better team. She was going to have the chance to play her heart out during the game.

On the next serve, the Blazes returned the ball. A Rockets player got the ball over to Beth.

Ella was in perfect position for the spike. Beth was in the center of the court, facing directly at Ella.

It should be an easy set for the spike. But instead of setting the ball up for Ella, Beth played the ball backward, over her head.

Gretchen was behind Ella, and she leaped up for the kill. She slammed the ball to the ground on the other side of the court. The Rockets led 6–0.

Ella was surprised that Beth hadn't set the ball to her. But since the play had turned out well, she didn't think much of it.

After a few more plays, however, Ella began to feel mad.

Every time the ball came to Beth for a set, she played the ball directly to Gretchen.

It didn't matter where anyone else was on the court. The ball always went to Gretchen.

Gretchen was a good player, so she usually scored a point. Sometimes, though, Gretchen was not in the best position to receive the pass. Then the spike attempts missed the mark, giving points to the Blazes.

As the game moved on, Beth and Gretchen made more and more mistakes. The other girls tried to get in, but Beth seemed to block them.

Finally, Coach Stiggle called a time out.

"What's going on out there?" she asked as the girls crowded around her.

No one responded. "Come on, you two, spill it," she said, looking directly at Beth and Gretchen.

Neither one of them said a word.

"Okay," Coach Stiggle said. "Get back out there. And play like a team."

CHAPTER 7
The Problem Grows

The team went back out on the court. But none of the players talked to each other. They all looked upset.

The tension made everyone play badly. Beth spread her passes around a little more, but she still sent most of her passes to Gretchen.

The Rockets were strong enough that they were able to carry the team to a couple of wins.

They made it to the championship match of the tournament.

Most of the team was unhappy, though. They weren't playing as a team, so even winning wasn't much fun.

When they went out on the court for the championship match, everyone but Beth and Gretchen looked sad.

No one tried to hurry through their warm-ups, and no one smiled. Except Beth and Gretchen. They seemed to be having a good time.

Before the match started, Coach Stiggle called the team together. "All right girls, here we go!" she said.

She looked at each girl in turn, smiling at each of them. She frowned when none of the girls smiled back.

Then she went on, "This is our first chance to win a tournament this year. I know you guys have it in you. Now let's go out there, have some fun, and play the best we can!" She smiled widely.

Instead of cheering like they usually did, the girls just mumbled and walked onto the court. Ella didn't even feel like playing anymore.

On the first few points of the game, Beth tried to set the ball only to Gretchen.

One of the sets went directly out of bounds. One was a good set that Gretchen spiked for a kill. Beth's third set was way off target and went out of bounds.

Two of those three plays would have been better if Beth had set the ball toward Ella instead.

The Rockets started to argue with each other. Then Beth set the ball over the top of Ella's head to get it to Gretchen.

Ella was really mad. "That's it!" Ella yelled. "Are you ever going to set the ball to anyone else?"

Beth just glared at her.

Coach Stiggle hadn't heard, so nothing happened. Ella was so angry that her face felt hot.

The rest of the match didn't go any better. Beth kept forcing passes to Gretchen, leaving open teammates to stand and watch.

The Rockets played poorly as a team, and no one was surprised when they lost the match. No one talked in the locker room afterward.

The next two tournaments were full of losses too. Ella still wasn't getting the ball very often.

Gretchen and Beth were good enough to get the team through early-round matches, but the Rockets were not able to win a championship.

After a loss in the championship match of another tournament, Ella had finally had enough. In the locker room, she stormed over to Gretchen and Beth.

"Listen, you guys," Ella said, "we're never going to win a tournament if we don't play like a team."

"You don't know anything about winning," Beth snapped. "How many tournaments have you won? We won a bunch with the Lakers."

"That's because there were other good players on the Lakers, too, and you played as a team," Ella said. The other girls stared up at her. "It wasn't just you two," Ella went on. "No matter how good you are, we'll never win if you hog the ball."

CHAPTER 8
Laura's Return

At practice the next week, Gretchen and Beth refused to talk to Ella. But Ella didn't care, because Laura was back at practice! Her doctors had said that her knee was healed enough to play.

She and Ella were both thrilled. The other girls seemed happier, too. Having Laura back meant that the team might share the ball a little more. And maybe, just maybe, it would start to be more fun.

The next weekend's tournament was going to be one of the toughest ones of the season. It was a regional tournament, so teams were coming in from all over to compete for the championship.

At practice, Beth and Gretchen paired up to work on drills, and Ella stuck with Laura. It looked like the team might be even more divided than ever.

Before the tournament, Laura pulled Ella aside. "I have an idea," Laura said. "Let's give them a taste of their own medicine. Every time I get the ball, I'll set it to you, no matter where you are."

Ella thought about it for a minute. "No way," she said finally. "We have to play the way we normally would, if we want to have a chance to win."

"Why?" Laura asked. "We should treat them how they've been treating us. They've been treating you bad all season. Now they'll know how it feels."

Ella sighed. She was tempted. She'd hated being left out and feeling like the team was under the control of Beth and Gretchen.

On the other hand, though, she didn't think the Rockets could win a tournament without the whole team playing together.

"No, Laura," Ella said quietly. "It won't work. I'm sorry, but we have to play as a team if we're going to win."

The Rockets opened the tournament with a match against a team they had beaten many times. On the game's first point, the ball was sent to Laura for a set.

Gretchen was right in front of her, set up for an easy spike. And Laura came through, setting the ball perfectly to her.

Gretchen reacted slowly. She seemed a little surprised that the ball was coming her way. But she recovered, jumped high, and spiked the ball for a kill.

Laura ran right to her and extended her hand. "Nice kill!" Laura yelled. Gretchen slapped hands with her.

The rest of the match was easy. Laura set up all the hitters on the team for kills.

Beth still passed to Gretchen more than the others, but once in a while she did send the ball to other players for kills. The Rockets rolled to the victory.

After two more wins, the Rockets were headed to another championship match.

But then they realized something. They were scheduled to play against the Lakers.

As the teams headed out on the court for warm-ups, one of the Lakers players walked over to Ella and Laura.

"I see you've taken in our outcasts," the girl said, motioning to Gretchen and Beth. "They weren't ever good enough for the Lakers anyway."

Gretchen and Beth overheard the comment. They started to walk over to the Lakers player. Both of them had angry looks on their faces. But Ella stopped them.

"Really?" Ella said. "We think they're great teammates. And they've been a great addition to our team. In our next match, you're going to find out just how good they really are."

The Lakers player stared at her and walked away. Gretchen and Beth looked at Ella. They couldn't believe what they had heard. They were speechless.

Ella smiled at them. "Are you ready to beat them?" she asked. "I sure am."

Gretchen and Beth, still a little stunned, nodded. Then all three girls jogged out onto the court.

The match was quick and easy for the Rockets. Beth and Laura fed their teammates all over the court for easy kills. They shared the ball, and they shared the credit.

Ella and Gretchen both had dozens of kills. The Rockets won the first two games.

At the end of the third game, the score was tied. Ella had the serve.

"Come on, Ella, you can do it!" Gretchen shouted.

Ella knew what to do.

Thud. Thud. She bounced the ball twice. Then she held it out in front of her in her left hand. She stared it down.

Then she pulled it back in and bounced it twice more. *Thud. Thud.*

Finally, she charged forward and flipped the ball into the air. She pounded a jump serve across the net.

It landed perfectly between the other team's players for an ace.

The Rockets rushed to the middle of the court and celebrated together.

Ella couldn't stop smiling.

ABOUT THE AUTHOR

Bob Temple lives in Rosemount, Minnesota, with his wife and three children. He has written more than thirty books for children. Over the years, he has coached more than twenty kids' soccer, basketball, and baseball teams. He also loves visiting classrooms to talk about his writing.

ABOUT THE ILLUSTRATOR

When Tuesday Mourning was a little girl, she knew she wanted to be an artist when she grew up. Now she is an illustrator who lives in Knoxville, Tennessee. She especially loves illustrating books for kids and teenagers. When she isn't illustrating, Tuesday loves spending time with her husband, who is an actor, and their son, Atticus.

GLOSSARY

championship (CHAM-pee-uhn-ship)—a contest that determines a winner

competition (com-puh-TISH-uhn)—a contest

congratulate (kuhn-GRACH-uh-late)—to tell someone that you are glad that they did well

control (kuhn-TROHL)—to make something do what you want

ignore (ig-NOR)—take no notice of something

ligaments (LIG-uh-muhnt)—the tough band of tissue that connects bones

physical therapy (FIZ-uh-kuhl THAIR-uh-pee)—the treatment of injured muscles

powerful (POU-ur-fuhl)—having great strength

rivals (RYE-vuhlz)—someone you're competing against

target (TAR-git)—a goal or an aim

tension (TEN-shuhn)—a strain in a relationship

threat (THRET)—a warning

tournament (TUR-nuh-muhnt)—a series of contests

VOLLEYBALL WORDS

ace (AYSS)—a serve that cannot be passed by the receiving team

assist (uh-SIST)—passing or setting the ball to a teammate who spikes the ball for a kill

block (BLOK)—a defensive play in which a player deflects a spike by the other team

bump (BUHMP)—to pass the ball with your forearms

dig (DIG)—to pass a spiked or rapidly hit ball, saving it from hitting the floor

foul (FOUL)—a violation of the rules

hit (HIT)—to jump and strike the ball with an overhand, forceful shot

hitter (HIT-tur)—the player who spikes the ball over the net

YOU SHOULD KNOW

jump serve (JUHMP SURV)—a serve in which the server tosses the ball into the air, jumps, and hits the ball over the net

kill (KIL)—a spike that results in a point

outside hitter (OUT-side HIT-tur)—a position played from the left or right front spot on the court. These players take most of the spikes in a game.

serve (SURV)—to put the ball into play at the start of a point.

set (SET)—to play the ball up into the air, near the net, so that it can be spiked

setter (SET-tur)—the player who sets the ball for a teammate to hit

spike (SPIKE)—a forceful hit designed to drive the ball to the floor on the opponent's side of the net

DISCUSSION QUESTIONS

1. When Gretchen and Beth joined the Rockets, they were rude to their new teammates. How should they have acted? What could Ella and Laura have done to help make the Rockets more of a team after Gretchen and Beth joined?

2. When Laura got hurt, Ella was more concerned with helping her off the court than with shaking hands with the other team. The Lakers said she was a bad loser. What do you think? What would you have done?

3. Some of the girls in this book call names and tease other girls as a way to help them win. What do you think about that?

WRITING PROMPTS

1. Near the end of this book, Laura tries to get Ella to play selfishly. Have you ever acted selfish or seen someone act selfish during a game? What happened? Write about it.

2. Laura is really upset when she gets hurt and isn't able to play. Have you ever had to sit out from your favorite sport for any reason? What happened? How did you feel? What did you do about it?

3. Ella has been perfecting her jump serve. Choose your favorite sport, and pick something you'd like to learn how to do in that sport. What is it? Why do you want to learn that? Write about it!

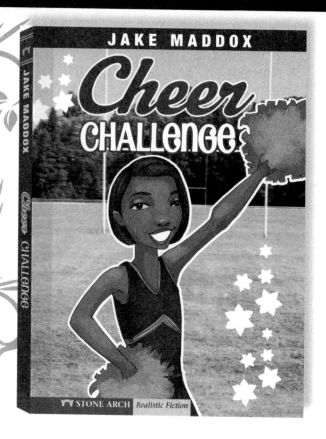

JAKE MADDOX

Cheer CHALLENGE

STONE ARCH *Realistic Fiction*

Being captain of the cheerleading squad is harder than Amanda thought. Can she figure out how to inspire the rest of the squad in time to make it to the biggest cheerleading competition of her life?

BY JAKE MADDOX

JAKE MADDOX

FULL COURT Dreams

STONE ARCH *Realistic Fiction*

Annie's been practicing her heart out in order to make the basketball team this year. But as she tries out, things keep going wrong. Can she take the pressure, do her best, and make the team? Annie won't let anything stand in her way!

INTERNET SITES

Do you want to know more about subjects related to this book? Or are you interested in learning about other topics? Then check out FactHound, a fun, easy way to find Internet sites.

Our investigative staff has already sniffed out great sites for you!

Here's how to use FactHound:

1. Visit *www.facthound.com*

2. Select your grade level.

3. To learn more about subjects related to this book, type in the book's ISBN number: **9781434204707**.

4. Click the **Fetch It** button.

FactHound will fetch the best Internet sites for you!